With special thanks to Allan Frewin

www.beastquest.co.uk

ORCHARD BOOKS
338 Euston Road, London NW1 3BH
Orchard Books Australia
Level 17/207 Kent St, Sydney, NSW 2000

A Paperback Original
First published in Great Britain in 2008

Beast Quest is a registered trademark of Beast Quest Limited
Series created by Working Partners Limited, London

Text © Working Partners Limited 2008
Cover illustration © David Wyatt 2008
Inside illustrations © Orchard Books 2008

A CIP catalogue record for this book is available
from the British Library.

ISBN 978 1 84616 951 9

16

Printed and bound by CPI Group (UK) Ltd, Croydon, CR0 4YY

The paper and board used in this paperback are natural recyclable
products made from wood grown in sustainable forests. The
manufacturing processes conform to the environmental regulations of
the country of origin.

Orchard Books is a division of Hachette Children's Books,
an Hachette UK company.

www.hachette.co.uk

VEDRA & KRIMON
TWIN BEASTS OF AVANTIA

BY ADAM BLADE

ORCHARD BOOKS

THE PIT OF

MALVEL'S M

THE NIDREM CAVES

THE RIVER DOUR

KING
HUGO'S
PALACE

THE CITY

TWIN BEASTS

*W*elcome to Avantia. I am Aduro – a good wizard residing in the palace of King Hugo. You join us to witness the birth of twin Beasts, the dragons Vedra and Krimon.

The new Beasts must make the journey to the neighbouring kingdom of Rion, where they can grow up in safety. But the evil wizard Malvel is never far away and the young twins need protecting. Accompanied by Ferno the fire dragon and Epos the flame bird, Tom will join the twin Beasts' journey. Only he can fend off their enemies, because Ferno and Epos cannot attack. Like the other good Beasts of Avantia, they can only protect. So Tom may be needed to fight fiercely.

Can Tom protect Vedra and Krimon, the twin Beasts of Avantia? We sincerely hope so.

Avantia salutes you,

Aduro

CHAPTER ONE

A NEW PERIL

Tom patted his brave stallion on the neck.

"Get well soon, Storm," he murmured. Tom's horse had been lamed on a rock, but was healing well in the palace stables. His friend Elenna's pet wolf, Silver, lay in the straw at Storm's side, refusing to leave. "I have to go now," Tom told the animals. "But I'll come and see you again as soon as I can."

Tom left the stables, gazing up at the tall purple spires and sea-green domes of the Royal Palace. The towns and villages, fields and forests of Avantia were white with late winter snow. But in the Great Hall of the palace, a party was taking place to celebrate King Hugo's birthday.

Tom took a seat beside Elenna, who was sitting on a bench with her bow and quiver of arrows at her side. The hall was full of people eating and dancing to the music.

"A toast!" called one of the royal courtiers. "To King Hugo: long may he reign!" There was a roar of approval and everyone raised their glasses.

Tom felt a rush of pride that he was a friend to the noble king. Elenna smiled and tapped her goblet against his. Then she leaned over and whispered into Tom's ear. "And to the six Beasts of Avantia!"

"Shhh!" warned Tom. As far as most of the people of Avantia knew, the Beasts were just legend. It was the greatest secret in the realm that the old stories about six Beasts that protected the land were true! Tom and Elenna had seen the Beasts. And more than that – they had freed them from the evil power of the wizard Malvel.

But as Tom looked along the table, he thought it was strange that Aduro, the good wizard of Avantia, did not seem to be enjoying the party. The elderly man sat silently in his chair, wrapped in his faded blue and red silk robes, his face solemn and his hand stroking his wispy grey beard.

The wizard turned and his grey eyes stared straight into Tom's.

"You are right," Aduro said with a grim smile. "I am troubled."

Tom had forgotten the wizard's power to read minds. Aduro pushed his chair back, rose and came over to them. He rested his hands on Tom's and Elenna's shoulders.

"Come with me," he said quietly. "I have something to tell you."

They got up from the table. Aduro parted a tapestry curtain and they slipped quietly out of the hall through a doorway. They found themselves in a little room with tall windows that looked out over the snow-covered town. Night had fallen and the sky was bright with the glow of watch fires.

"Has something bad happened?" Elenna asked. "Are the Beasts in danger?"

Aduro gave her a mysterious look. "The Beasts you saved from Malvel's evil power are safe. But, elsewhere in our realm, something strange and wonderful has taken place. Something that happens only once in a thousand years." He leaned close, his eyes sparkling. "The forces that rule our world have created two new Beasts."

Tom gasped. "I didn't even know that was possible," he said. "What kind of Beast are they?"

"Twin dragons, Vedra and Krimon," Aduro said. "Hatched from a single egg that lay hidden for centuries in the Nidrem Caves."

"Baby dragons!" Elenna breathed. "Will we ever get to see them?"

The wizard's face was solemn. "That is why I brought you here." He drew himself up to his full height. "The birth of Vedra and Krimon could put the kingdom of Avantia in terrible danger once more."

He closed his hand around the jewel that hung from a thick chain about his neck. Tom saw a blue light shining out from between his fingers. The light hit the wall of the chamber. In the circle of light, Tom could see that the wizard had conjured a vision.

It showed a dark cave of sharp black rocks. At the back of the cave,

they could make out the broken
shards of a thick white egg – an egg
that must have been the size of
a wagon when it was whole. Curious
shapes lay curled on the floor
of the cave.

"I can't make it out," Tom said, peering at the magical scene. "What are those green and red things?"

"Can't you guess?" Elenna said. "It's the dragons!"

"Oh! Yes!" Tom gazed at the dragons curled up together, their wings and tails and long necks wrapped around one another. Their eyes were closed and thin streams of smoke drifted from their nostrils. He felt his heart lift at the sight of the newborn Beasts. They were magnificent and precious all at once. "Which one is Vedra and which one is Krimon?" he asked.

"Vedra is the green dragon and Krimon is the red dragon," Aduro replied. He took his hand away from the jewel and the vision faded. "It is rare for two Beasts to be created at the same time. And, at this age, they

18

are at their most vulnerable. If Malvel learns of their existence, he will do everything in his power to corrupt them and use them for his evil purposes."

"We'll protect them," Tom vowed.

"We'll do whatever it takes!" Elenna added hotly.

Aduro smiled. "I hoped you would say that," he continued. "But I must warn you, this will be a dangerous quest, unlike any you have undertaken. You must be sure that you are up to the task."

Tom and Elenna looked at one another for a moment then turned to the wizard.

"We are!" they said together.

CHAPTER TWO

THE DARK RIVER

The wizard led Tom and Elenna through a side-door and down a long winding stone stairway lit by flaming torches. Down and down the stairs went, and Tom realised with excitement that Aduro was taking them to the cellars that lay deep under the palace.

At last, the stairs ended and they followed the wizard through a series of dark cellar rooms while the sounds of the celebrations far above them faded away. Finally they came to a locked door. Aduro lifted his jewel pendant and touched it against the wood. The door sprang open.

He took a torch from the wall and led them into the room. It was small and round and quite bare except for a gigantic wooden chest with metal straps that stood in the middle of the stone floor. A bundle of cloth lay beside the chest, and next to it were Tom's shield and sword, along with Elenna's bow and quiver of arrows. Aduro must have magically brought them here, ready and waiting for them.

Tom looked around.

"Why have you brought us here?" he asked. "There's no way out."

Aduro looked at him and smiled.

"Isn't there?" he said.

The wizard walked over to the chest and made a movement with his hand over the curved lid. It flew open with a loud, startling clank.

Aduro picked up the bundle of cloth and then climbed into the chcst. "Come, bring your things," he said. "Both of you – join me."

Puzzled, Tom picked up his sword and the magic shield. It was decorated with powerful tokens from each of his previous quests. It could protect him from fire and even heal all wounds. He climbed into the chest beside the wizard, leaving room for Elenna to follow him with her bow and arrows.

Aduro stamped his foot twice and a panel in the bottom of the chest slid away to reveal a stone stairway that led down into utter darkness.

The wizard began to descend. Tom and Elenna exchanged a brief look and then followed.

Torch flames shone on the walls of the narrow stairway. Their footsteps echoed, but Tom could hear another sound. It was coming from below, an odd, rushing noise that he thought he recognised.

Dampness oozed from the walls, making the stones shine eerily in the firelight.

"That noise – it's running water!" Tom exclaimed.

"It is the hidden River Dour," announced Aduro, as they came to the end of the steps. They found themselves by a wide, rushing underground river of black water.

"This river will take you to the very heart of the Nidrem Caves, the sacred place where the Beasts gather and where none but the Master of the Beasts has ever set foot."

Tom had heard of the Nidrem Caves, but they were the most sacred place in all of Avantia and he had never expected to go there. He frowned, realising that they would have to go on this quest without Storm and Silver. "Will you come with us?" he asked the wizard.

"This is your destiny, not mine," said Aduro. "You and Elenna must journey to the Nidrem Caves on your own."

Aduro led them along the rocky riverbank until they came to a place where a small rowing boat was moored.

"The River Dour will lead you

to the caves where the dragons hatched," the wizard told them. "Once there you must take Vedra and Krimon north, into the mountainous kingdom of Rion. There they will be safe from the evil reach of Malvel." His eyes glittered in the light thrown by the flaming torches. "But beware – if the dragons are not taken to safety before the rise of the full moon, Malvel will be able to cast his wicked spell on them."

"But what if Malvel gets to them first?" asked Tom. "Is there anything we can do to break the spell?"

"That would not be easy," Aduro said. "Let me see your sword."

Tom drew his sword from his belt and handed it to Aduro. This sword had helped him on so many adventures. It shone brightly in the flickering light. Aduro gazed at it

solemnly, then drew the blade up
to his lips and whispered a few
words. Tom's fingers tingled at the
sound of the strange chant.

"Your sword is now enchanted,"
Aduro said. "If Malvel puts an evil
spell on the twin Beasts, the only
way to set them free is for you
to score their tender underbellies
with the tip of your blade." He
looked at Tom. "It will take only
a single touch, a light stroke, enough
to scar but not to wound. That will
serve as a symbol of good. Only the

steadiest of hands can make such
a cut, and it must be done before the
full moon has reached the very top
of the sky...otherwise Malvel's spell
will be unbreakable and Vedra and
Krimon will be corrupted for ever
and become Beasts of evil."

"I can do it," Tom said.

Aduro nodded. "Now, my friends,"
he said. "It's time to go."

Tom and Elenna climbed down
into the bobbing boat. The rush of
running water was all around them.

"Take this," Aduro said, handing
down the bundle. "It is food and
drink for your long journey – and
warm cloaks to keep out the cold.
I know that your shield has Nanook
the snow monster's bell on it
to protect you from cold, Tom, but
the cloak will save you from getting
soaked to the skin if it snows."

"Thank you, Aduro," Tom said, placing the bundle in the bottom of the boat.

"Farewell," said Aduro. "May your quest be successful."

Tom looked up at the wizard from the prow of the boat. "While there is blood in my veins, I shall do all that I can to keep Vedra and Krimon safe!" he vowed solemnly.

"And so will I!" Elenna added, her eyes flashing.

"Then go, my brave friends," said the wizard, handing them a torch. He loosened the rope that held the boat to the shore.

Elenna set the flickering torch in a holder in the prow. Tom used a paddle to bring the little craft out onto the centre of the dark river and handed the other paddle to Elenna so that she could help him row.

A sound came to their ears, booming in the distance like sinister, mocking laughter.

"Malvel?" Elenna muttered.

"Yes, I think so," Tom said quietly. He shivered. The River Dour was leading them into who knew what deadly dangers.

"Will we succeed again?" Elenna mused anxiously. "Can we defeat Malvel a second time?"

Tom stared out over the prow of the boat.

"Don't worry," he said, trying to reassure her. "We've never failed before – and we're not going to fail now!"

CHAPTER THREE

THE TWIN DRAGONS

The river churned all around them. They had been swept along on the dark water for hours.

"Oh no!" Elenna said, peering forward. Tom looked. There was a thin line of white in the water. The noise of the river had become louder and more urgent.

"Rocks!" Tom gasped. "And the

current is pulling us towards them!"

The two friends dug their paddles into the water, fighting to turn the boat away from the path of the rocks. Sweat ran down Tom's face, his muscles aching as he thrust the paddle into the water over and over again. Tom knew that the splinter of Sepron's tooth that was fitted to his shield worked as a protection against fast-flowing water – but he wasn't so sure it could save him and Elenna from these rocks! They were very close now. He could see their edges glistening in the light of the torch flame.

"Come on!" Tom shouted. "We can do this!" He wasn't going to lose heart so early in the quest. Gradually, the boat began to turn.

"We did it!" Elenna cheered as the first of the rocks slid by. But there were more sharp black rocks stabbing upwards out of the swirling water. White foam broke against them as the river tried to dash the boat to pieces.

They paddled furiously, and at last they came through the rocks and were able to get their breath back.

"I hope this river doesn't have any more nasty surprises for us!" Tom gasped.

Far ahead, they became aware of a faint light – not daylight, but a soft blue glow that was like a steady flame.

As the light grew, they were able to make out the banks of the river and the ridged stone roof high above their heads. The blue light played on the water, getting brighter and brighter.

Their boat floated gently into a wide, calm lake under a high dome of rock.

"The light is coming from the rocks," Tom said. "And look! There's something in the water." He pointed.

A large shape was cutting through

the lake, sending up spouts of white foam. They recognised the Beast at once.

"It's Sepron!" Elenna shouted joyfully. The huge sea serpent was snaking through the water towards them, his scaly green body crested with a long fin and his seaweed-like mane streaming back from his head.

He opened his massive jaws and let out a deep bellowing cry of welcome.

"Hello, Sepron!" Tom shouted. The Beast was huge. He swam around the boat, surrounding it with his long shining coils. Then they saw the other Beasts gathered together on the shore.

Arcta the mountain giant came striding out into the water, his massive body covered in thick shaggy hair, his face peering down at them.

"Careful, Arcta!" Tom shouted up. "You'll swamp the boat."

None of the Beasts could speak, but Arcta gave a grunt as though he knew what Tom meant. He leaned down and gently picked up Tom and Elenna, then turned and waded back to the shore, putting his friends down carefully on firm ground.

The huge fire dragon Ferno lay under a cliff, his black wings folded along his back, smoke drifting from

his nostrils, his red eyes friendly. Nanook the snow monster shambled forwards, making welcoming snuffling sounds as she squatted down in front of the two friends. She reached out her two great hairy arms and pulled them into her snow-white fur. It felt to Tom as if he was being wrapped in a huge fleecy blanket until Nanook let them go again.

There was a loud croaking behind them and they found themselves staring up into the fiery eyes of Epos the flame bird.

A mighty clopping of hooves announced the approach of Tagus the horse-man. He reached down to Tom and Elenna, lifted them up and placed them onto his broad back.

He made a sound that was half-speech and half-neighing, and then he went cantering off along the

glowing blue shore of the great
underground lake with Tom and
Elenna clinging to his back.

"Hang on tight!" Tom called
to Elenna. He looked back and saw that
the other Beasts were following. It felt
good to be surrounded by all of his
extraordinary and powerful friends.

They quickly came to a large cave. A little way off, the cave's floor sloped upwards and they could see daylight – it was the way out of the Nidrem Caves! Tom and Elenna jumped down from Tagus's back.

The two newborn dragons lay together in a nest of golden straw. One was emerald green, the other red as a ruby. Their trusting eyes gazed at Tom and Elenna, white steam rising from their nostrils.

"That's why the Beasts are all here together," Tom said to Elenna. "They're protecting Vedra and Krimon."

Even newly hatched, the two Beasts were twice Tom's height as he approached them.

"We're here to help you," he said soothingly. He realized they didn't know what he was saying, but the Beasts often seemed to understand the meaning behind his words.

Vedra let out a nervous hiccup of excitement and a small spurt of red fire belched from between his jaws.

"Oh! They're lovely!" Elenna said, reaching out her arms to the Beasts. The two dragons clambered out of the straw and moved forwards unsteadily, their wings scraping the ground, their necks stretching out as they made little sounds in their throats.

Tom patted the hard shining scales on Vedra's neck, allowing the Beast to nuzzle up against him. He was aware of a faint burning smell, like the smouldering embers of a fire. He felt awed by the baby dragons, but also strangely protective of them. He knew it was his duty to keep them safe!

Krimon was standing in front of Elenna, gently pecking at her hair, a low rumbling sound coming from his belly, as if he was purring in contentment.

"They're so trusting!" Elenna said, looking at Tom with concern. "Malvel mustn't be allowed anywhere near them!"

Tom looked at the other Beasts, gathered in the mouth of the cave.

He turned to Elenna. "Do you think they know what we have to do?" he said.

"Even if they do, how are we going to get the dragons to Rion?" Elenna asked. "How far is it – and how will we know when we're there?"

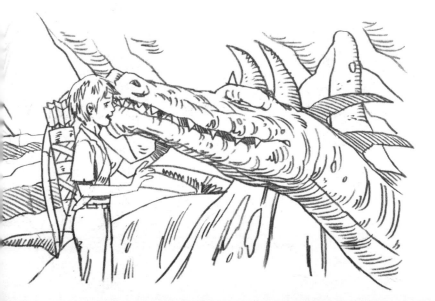

Before Tom could reply, he felt
a tingling against his chest. Puzzled,
he drew out the magic parchment
map Aduro had given him when he
started his very first quest. It wasn't
flat like an ordinary map – it was
alive! Snow-covered mountains rose
up in sharp points from the
parchment and Tom knew that if he
touched the blue threads of the
rivers, his fingers would be wet. The
map had led the way to all his
previous adventures, spinning out
paths to guide him.

There was something new on the
map! To the north of the palace, it
glowed with a tiny point of golden
light. He looked closer. The light was
the cave mouth, and from it
a slender golden path was spreading
out, pointing the way north.

As he watched, the northern limits

of the map began to expand beyond the boundaries of Avantia. New mountains rose up from the white parchment. There were new rivers and forests as well, and Tom realised that the map was changing to show him the snowy land of Rion.

He frowned. "It's a long way," he said.

"And Malvel could be following us," Elenna agreed.

Tom shivered. How could they possibly hope to get all the way to Rion without the evil wizard tracking them down and putting a spell on the young Beasts? And time was not on their side. The full moon was going to rise tonight – if Vedra and Krimon were not hidden in Rion by then, he would have failed in his quest.

Aduro had been right – this was going to be their greatest challenge yet!

CHAPTER FOUR

FLYING NORTH

Tom looked at Elenna. "We should go – as quickly as possible."

"I'll get the rest of the food and the cloaks Aduro gave us," Elenna called as she leapt onto Tagus's back and galloped off to the boat.

Tom looked at the baby dragons. They were sitting quietly on their haunches, watching him with curious, innocent eyes.

"Please try to understand me," Tom said. "You must come with us. You will be in terrible danger if you stay here." They blinked at him. "There is an evil wizard who wishes to hurt you!" Tom continued.

Vedra and Krimon shifted uneasily, as though they sensed the urgency in Tom's voice.

Tom tapped his hand against his chest. "I am here to protect you."

"We are here to protect them,

you mean," said Elenna, riding up
behind him with the bundled cloaks
in her arms. "Well, let's see if they
understand," she added, hopping off
the horse-man. "Come on, little
dragons – follow us!" She began
to walk in the direction of the mouth
of the cave.

To Tom's delight, the baby dragons
got up and began to walk along
behind them. The other Beasts
followed, too.

They soon arrived at the wide cave mouth and found themselves staring out over a landscape of snow-covered hills and forests. This was a part of the kingdom Tom had never seen before.

The sky was clear and the dawning sun was low on the eastern horizon. Tom knew they must already be a long way from the Royal Palace, but the map showed that they still had a great distance to travel.

Tom and Elenna put their cloaks on. Sepron had stayed in the lake, but the other Beasts were congregated around them, as if to say farewell.

"We have to go now," Tom said to the Beasts.

Ferno and Epos stepped forwards.

"What is it?" Elenna asked. Arcta picked her up, and Nanook picked Tom up. Tom's head spun as he was swung up onto Epos's feathery back. Elenna was placed astride Ferno's scaly neck.

"Of course!" Tom said. "They know we don't have much time to get to Rion. It would be impossible to fulfil the quest without them!"

"But what about Vedra and Krimon?" Elenna said. "I know they've got wings, but we can't expect them to fly all the way, they're far too young."

Ferno turned his vast head to where Vedra and Krimon stood and made some deep rumbling sounds in his throat.

The baby dragons moved at once, Krimon clambering awkwardly up Ferno's wing onto the great dragon's back behind Elenna, and Vedra climbing onto Epos's back, cuddling up into the long warm feathers just behind where Tom sat.

With a heavy flapping of wings, Ferno and Epos rose into the air. The snowy landscape fell away beneath them. Ferno and Epos circled the cave mouth where the other Beasts stood, proudly gazing up at them.

"Goodbye!" Tom called, reaching

around to check that his shield was firmly in place on his back. The next moment, he needed both hands to cling to Epos's feathers as the great bird made a long curving swing upwards and northwards. Tom looked over his shoulder. Vedra was

pressed tight onto Epos's back, his
eyes wide with wonder as he stared
down at the passing countryside.

"Malvel won't catch us now!"
Elenna called.

"I hope not!" Tom called back.

They flew silently over the wintry
landscape, the smooth blanket
of snow shining like silver under the
sun. It was early afternoon when Tom
saw high mountains approaching
under a sky thick with snow-clouds.

Soon they were beneath the
clouds, flying through the snow that
filled the sky. Their breath came out
as mist, but Aduro's cloaks kept them
snug and warm.

They flew over a jagged-toothed
region of hills and crags. Tom pulled
out the map and cleared the
snowflakes out of his eyes. A golden
glow showed their position. They

were still in Avantia, but the border of Rion was fast approaching. It would not be long now!

Then Tom saw something odd on the map. He brought the parchment up closer to his face. One of the mountains on the map was different to all the others. It had a crater that was glowing with a fierce red fire.

"There's something strange ahead!" Elenna called.

Tom lifted his eyes. Right in front of them was the mountain that he had been looking at on the map.

"It's a volcano!" Tom shouted. "And it's erupting right in front of us!"

Epos let out a croak of alarm as a flood of molten rock and boiling smoke gushed up into the air. Tom saw that Elenna and Krimon were only just able to hold onto Ferno's back as he swerved away to the left to avoid the scalding fountain of fire.

A moment later Tom was almost wrenched from his place as Epos tried to avoid the huge flaming lumps of rock that were coming down in a deadly fiery rain. Vedra cried out behind him, clinging on fiercely to Epos's feathers.

Tom saw a fiery thunderbolt plunging towards them. He leaned back towards the baby dragon, throwing his shield up above his head in a desperate attempt to save them both.

Was the quest going to end before it had begun?

CHAPTER FIVE

THE BOY ON THE MOUNTAIN

The red-hot thunderbolt bounced off Tom's shield, hissing and spitting. The magical dragon scale in the shield had saved them! Tom's arm ached, but he kept the shield steady, while Vedra cowered behind him, shivering and whimpering in fright.

Tom saw Elenna clutching onto Ferno, with the other terrified baby dragon squawking behind her as the huge Beast struggled to get clear of the volcano. But as Ferno turned, Tom saw Elenna's bow and quiver of arrows fall, spinning downwards until they were lost in the flaming crater.

Epos gave a caw of alarm as she tried to pull back from the fiery mountain. The bird's body tilted as she swung away. Tom felt himself slipping. He had been so intent on keeping Vedra safe from the rain of fiery rock that he was not holding on tightly enough. He scrabbled for a handhold as he slipped from Epos's back.

"No!" he cried. The sky and the mountains wheeled around him. He saw Epos above him, her wings beating fiercely.

I've failed, Tom thought as he plunged helplessly downwards.

A wild rushing sound filled his ears,

like a racing wind. Moments later, all the
breath was jolted from his body. Epos
had swooped under him, catching him
with a triumphant shriek.

Tom gasped, dizzy from his rescue. Dazed, he crawled up to sit between Epos's wings. "Thank you!" he shouted. He looked over his shoulder. The green dragon was nodding his head and making chirping noises, glad that Tom had been rescued.

Ferno came swooping close.

"I lost my bow and arrows," Elenna called unhappily. "I can't believe they're gone!"

"Yes, I saw," Tom shouted. "It can't be helped. Let's get away from this volcano – then we can take a rest and work out what we're going to do."

They flew on until the red glow of the volcano was far behind them. Tom peered down, scouring the rugged landscape for somewhere to land.

"Down there!" he called, pointing to a large flat slab of rock on a low ridge between the mountains.

Epos and Ferno circled down and landed. Tom spotted something at the far end of the slab of rock – something small and curled up – a sleeping animal, maybe.

He jumped down from Epos's back and went over to investigate. Elenna followed. "What is it?" she asked.

"It's a boy!" gasped Tom, stopping in surprise a few steps away from the curled-up shape. "What's he doing here all on his own?"

"Let's find out," Elenna said, running ahead of Tom.

"Be careful," Tom warned. He could hear an uneasy rumbling in Ferno's throat, and Epos was cawing nervously. Vedra and Krimon were staring at the boy and shivering. Something was wrong. The boy was only wearing light clothing, but the wind was raw and cut to the bone. How could he be sleeping in such a remote place as this? It didn't make sense.

"I don't think you should wake him," Tom said, coming up behind Elenna. "We have to get going." But Elenna crouched at the boy's side and shook his shoulder.

"Hey! Are you all right?"

The boy's blue eyes snapped open and he jumped to his feet, his icy gaze strangely alert in his gaunt, pale face. Elenna stumbled back in surprise at the sudden movement. The boy stared at Tom, his lips spreading into a thin smile.

Tom looked at him. Those eyes were oddly familiar. As they stood staring at one another, cold threads of mist curled across the barren rock, making Tom shudder.

"My name is Seth," the boy said, his smile widening as he thrust out a hand towards Tom. "Who are you?"

Uncertainly, Tom reached out his own hand. "I'm Tom, and this is—"

He got no further. The boy's eyes flashed and his smile turned to a grimace as he lunged forwards, grabbing Tom's arm with both hands.

Tom let out a yell of shock as Seth half-turned, pulling Tom's arm so that he staggered off-balance and was thrown headlong over the boy's shoulder.

With a cry of pain, he came crashing down onto a rock on his back. He felt dizzy and disorientated and his eyes swam. He heard Elenna shout something.

He stared up at the white sky, gasping for breath. Seth loomed over him, and Tom saw that he had a bronze sword in his hand, the point aiming for Tom's throat.

"And now that we have been introduced," the boy snarled. "I'm going to kill you!"

Tom stared up, helpless, as the blade rose and then plunged down towards him.

CHAPTER SIX

MAGIC DUST

Tom twisted to one side as the point of the bronze sword struck the rock close to his head, filling his eyes with sparks. Seth grunted with frustration as he stumbled forwards. Tom sprang quickly to his feet, drawing his own sword and turning to face his foe, his shield up to defend himself.

"Why are you attacking me?" Tom asked, but Seth had spun on his heel.

Bringing his blade up, he lunged forward with a snarl.

Tom used his sword to turn aside Seth's blade so that he could come in under the boy's arm and throw him off-balance with a thrust from his shield. But Seth was too good a swordsman to be defeated by such a simple strategy. He bounded back, swinging his sword in a wide arc.

More sparks flew as their swords met with a clash, the noise echoing around the mountain peaks that surrounded them. Tom was aware

of Ferno moving closer and of Epos watching with bright, angry eyes.

"Watch out!" Elenna shouted as the bronze sword came slicing through the air at neck height. Tom fended it off with his shield and thrust hard with his own sword. Seth leapt to one side, beating at Tom's sword, almost smashing it from his grip.

Tom realised that Seth was his equal in strength, and a very dangerous fighter. He would have to do something unexpected if he was going to win.

Tom risked everything in one big gamble. He let Seth beat him back step after step across the rock. He could hear Ferno rumbling in concern as he gave the impression that he was weakening. Epos shrieked and Elenna let out a cry as Tom stumbled and fell onto his back.

Seth yelled in triumph and raised his sword high. But Tom had been faking his weakness. He twisted, scissoring his legs, and sliced Seth's feet from under him. Seth fell with a howl and Tom was up and on him in a moment. He kicked the bronze blade out of Seth's grip and stood over him, panting as he pointed his sword at the boy's throat.

"Oh! Well done, Tom!" Elenna shouted, running up to them. She stared down at the grimacing boy angrily. "Why did you do that? We weren't going to hurt you!"

The cold fire faded from Seth's eyes and a look of bewilderment came over him. "I'm so sorry!" he gasped, bringing his hands up over his face. "I didn't mean to hurt you. I didn't know what I was doing."

Tom glared down at him. "What are you talking about? You attacked me for no reason!"

"I was half-crazy with hunger and fear," said the boy. "I'm lost in this terrible place, and I haven't eaten for days. I thought you were a demon coming to murder me." He wiped his hand over his face. "I am truly sorry."

Tom frowned, confused by Seth's change of behaviour. "You really expect us to believe that you didn't know what you were doing?" he asked.

"Please," begged Seth, "I've been

hallucinating with hunger. I meant you no harm." He looked so pathetic and frail that Tom and Elenna exchanged a wary nod, deciding to give him another chance.

"All right," Elenna said. "Wait there. We have food and water." She ran over to Epos and pulled down their bag of provisions. Tom, still not quite certain that Seth's story was the truth, picked up the bronze sword and slipped it into his belt before he allowed Seth to climb to his feet.

"How did you get here?" Tom asked, eyeing the boy warily.

Seth tore into the loaf that Elenna had brought him, speaking with his mouth full. "I was with a hunting party – we were looking for the wild goats that live in these mountains. They make good eating. But a heavy fog came down and I got separated from the others. I've been surviving on rainwater and scraps of plants for days now." He looked gratefully at Elenna. "I thought I was going to die up here, all alone on this barren rock. You saved my life."

"You're welcome," Elenna said. She looked questioningly at Tom.

"I hope you find your way home safely," Tom said. "But we have to go now."

Seth gazed at the Beasts. "You fly on the most extraordinary...*birds*...I have ever seen," he said, his voice amazed. "At least, one of them is a bird, I think, huge though it is. But surely the other is a dragon?" A sudden light of understanding came into his eyes. "These must be two of the legendary Beasts of Avantia. They're *real*! Are you their Master?"

"No," Tom said, flattered that Seth might think that he could be the Master of the Beasts. "But I am their friend."

A smile spread across Seth's face. "I always thought in my heart that the legends were true," he said.

"No one is supposed to know," Elenna said. "The Beasts should never be seen."

Seth nodded. "Of course not," he said. He put his hand to his heart. "Don't worry," he said. "I promise that I will never tell anyone about

what I have seen in this place. On
my word of honour!" He looked
from Tom to Elenna. "But…I don't
know how to get down the
mountains from here. If you leave
me, I'll die."

"We can't take you with us," Tom
said. "We're on an important quest."

"We have to find the land of Rion,"
Elenna added.

"I live in Rion, in a small village beyond the mountains," Seth said. "Take me close to my home and I promise I will never speak of these magnificent Beasts to a living soul!"

Tom and Elenna looked uneasily at one another. Could they trust him? On the other hand, Tom thought, could they be so cruel as to leave him all alone in the mountains?

"You may ride with us," Tom said, making sure to add: "But only as far as your home village."

Seth bowed his head as if Tom were King Hugo. "Thank you."

They went back to where the Beasts were waiting. Tom climbed up onto Epos's back and reached down to help Seth up in front of him. He wanted to keep an eye on the mysterious boy. Vedra looked at the newcomer with curiosity. Seth reached out his hand as if to touch the Beast, but he belched a little fire and Seth snatched his hand back.

Soon they were airborne again, flying high over the mountains with the cool wind in their hair. Tom saw the landscape begin to change beneath them. The mountains gave way to rugged hills cloaked in snow-laden pine forests. Blue lakes glowed in the valleys and gushing rivers leaped from rock to rock in white waterfalls.

He took his map out. They were beyond the northern borders of Avantia now. For the first time in his life, Tom was outside his kingdom.

Epos turned her head as she surveyed the unfamiliar landscape. Tom could sense that the Beast was as unsure of this place as he was. As he looked to where Ferno was flying alongside, the anxious light in the dragon's eyes told a similar story.

"We're in Rion," Tom called to Elenna. "We must find somewhere safe to land!"

Beneath them stretched a great dense forest of pines. Tom searched for a clearing or open space where the Beasts could set down. Fierce snow-filled winds swept back and forth, making the tall pines bend and sway, and forcing Tom to cling tightly to Epos's back for fear of being blown off.

"There!" Elenna called, pointing down. "We can land there!"

Tom stared down. Yes! There was a clearing in the forest just ahead of them. Elenna and Ferno swooped down, and Epos prepared to follow.

Tom smiled. Aduro would be pleased with them – they had brought Vedra and Krimon to safety without any sign of Malvel.

But then Tom felt Seth shifting in front of him. He looked over Seth's shoulder and saw the boy take a small leather pouch out of his jacket.

"What is that?" Tom asked.

Seth opened the bag and dipped his hand into it. Golden powder trickled from between his fingers. "It's magic!" he said, that familiar cold light burning in his eyes again. "The dark and deadly magic of Malvel!"

"No!" Tom shouted. But he was too

late. Seth leaned forward and hurled
the fistful of gold dust into Epos's
eyes. The bird let out a deafening
croak of rage and alarm, twisting and
turning in the air.

Seth laughed and turned, hurling a second handful of dust into Tom's face. Tom was hanging onto Epos – he couldn't protect himself. The golden powder filled his eyes, stinging badly and blinding him. He clawed at his eyes, horribly aware of the air rushing wildly past him as Epos plummeted headlong towards the ground.

CHAPTER SEVEN

MALVEL'S LAUGHTER

Epos hit the ground with a crash that shook the forest. Tom plunged blindly from her back. As he fell, he could hear Vedra crying out and Epos croaking in pain and rage.

Tom rolled helplessly across the ground, losing his shield and sword as he tumbled over and over. At last, he came to a skidding halt in thick snow. He lay on his back, gasping and dizzy. A dancing golden light filled his stinging eyes, blotting everything else out.

"Elenna!" he called. *"Elenna!"*

He got to his feet, staggering blindly about, his hands hitting the trunks of trees, his nostrils filled with the scent of pine.

"I'm here!" called a familiar voice. "What happened? Did something hurt Epos?"

Tom grabbed hold of Elenna's arm. "It was Seth. He threw some dust in our eyes. It blinded us." Tom turned his head. "Where is he?" His voice was grim. "And where's my sword?"

"You can't fight him if you can't see," Elenna said, catching hold of Tom as he lurched towards the sound of Epos's caws. "Wait!" she said. "I can hear running water." She pushed Tom and he felt his back hit a tree trunk. "Stay right there!" she ordered, fumbling in her pocket for a handkerchief. "I'll get water to wash your eyes."

Tom stood listening to the sounds of the troubled Beasts – Epos's angry croaking and the anxious rumbling of Ferno. He could also hear the frightened cries of a baby dragon. How could he have been so stupid as to allow Seth to come along with them?

"I'm back!" It was Elenna's voice, and a moment later, icy water splashed in Tom's face. "Keep still," Elenna told him as Tom flinched away from the wet cloth. "There," she said. "How's that?"

Cautiously, Tom opened his eyes. There was still a golden glow on the edges of his vision, but the pain was gone and he could see again.

"Where is he?" Tom said angrily. He set off at a run back to the clearing where the Beasts waited. As he ran, he scooped up his sword and shield, readying himself for battle. He noticed that Seth's bronze sword was missing from his belt. That was bad. The boy was armed again; but this time, Tom would show him no mercy.

Epos was shaking her head from side to side, trying to get the golden dust out of her eyes. Ferno stood protectively close by, fire playing at his nostrils and his eyes glittering angrily.

There was no sign of Seth.

As Tom and Elenna raced into the clearing, Krimon came creeping out from where he had been hiding under Ferno's wing. He ran forwards, his wings flapping weakly.

Tom looked into the baby dragon's pleading eyes.

"Where's Vedra?" Elenna gasped, staring around the clearing.

"Seth must have taken him," Tom said. Filled with guilt and anger, he ran into the middle of the clearing, swinging his sword in his helpless rage. He shouted: "Seth! You dirty coward! Come back here and face me!"

A deep, hollow laugh echoed across the treetops. It was a horribly familiar sound that made Tom's flesh crawl. He came to a sudden stop, his anger freezing.

"*Malvel!*" he shouted into the air. "I swear, while there's blood in my veins, I'll get the Beast back from you!"

Another gust of laughter shivered through the trees.

Malvel had outwitted him, and now one of the twin Beasts was under the evil wizard's thrall.

Snow began to flurry across the clearing. Elenna came up behind Tom.

"We've failed," she murmured. "Malvel has beaten us."

"No!" Tom said firmly, gripping his sword. "We'll get Vedra back." He looked at her. "We will!"

But as the blizzard grew worse, his heart was filled with doubt. They were in an unknown land, and he had no idea how to start searching for the baby dragon. And there was still Krimon to protect. He wondered what new challenges awaited him.

DANGER IN RION

*W*elcome again to Avantia, my friends. I am Aduro the good wizard, addressing you once more from the palace of King Hugo. Tom and Elenna have been entrusted with the task of taking Vedra and Krimon, the two newborn Beasts, to safety in the snowy kingdom of Rion.

They have done well so far, taking the twin dragons all the way to Rion – but their quest is far from over! Malvel the evil wizard is close at hand, and his servant, the treacherous boy Seth, has stolen Vedra away.

Tom and Elenna have much to do! They must protect Krimon and rescue his brother – all before the full moon rises tonight. If they fail, then Malvel's evil influence will corrupt the twin dragons for all time!

Let us hope that good fortune is on their side.

Avantia salutes you,

Aduro

CHAPTER ONE

BLIZZARD

Tom stared grimly into the howling blizzard. How were they going to be able to track Seth and the lost Beast in such terrible weather?

Elenna stood at his side. "The full moon will rise tonight," she said thoughtfully. "We must rescue Vedra from Malvel before that."

Tom turned to look at Krimon, shivering at Ferno's side. Close by,

Epos was huddled on the ground.

"Will Epos be all right?" Elenna asked.

Tom ran over to the injured flame bird. "I hope so." He could see pain in the Beast's golden eyes. "But I don't think she'll be able to fly for a while."

Ferno crawled closer to Epos, lifting one black wing to shield the hurt bird from the blizzard. As the snow touched the great dragon's scaly hide, it turned to steam, so that the Beasts were shrouded in a cloud of fine mist. Krimon was huddled up against Ferno's side, mewling and staring around as though hoping that his brother would come trotting out of the snow at any moment.

Suddenly the red baby dragon let out a sharp cry and stood up. He scuttled forwards into the snow, making little calling sounds in his throat.

"Where's he going?" Elenna asked.

"I think he can sense his brother," Tom said.

Krimon headed towards the forest. He turned and looked back at Tom and Elenna. Then he lifted his head and let out a small spurt of flame from his mouth. His wing

lifted, beckoning to them.

Krimon turned to the forest again, tilting his head as though listening. He let out a high-pitched growl and darted forwards.

"We must follow him," Tom said.

"What about Epos and Ferno?" asked Elenna.

Tom turned and saw Ferno lift his black wing and curl it over Epos. Suddenly all that could be seen was a huge black rock in the

middle of the clearing.

"Just like when I first met him!" Tom said to Elenna. "Remember? He looked exactly like a part of the mountain. He's done the same thing again to keep them both safe." He turned to the forest. "I can't see Krimon any more. We mustn't lose him!"

Tom and Elenna plunged into the dark forest.

"Where has he gone?" Elenna asked, peering into the gloom.

Tom stared through the trees, but he could only see clearly for a little way, and after that, all was black and grim. There was no sign of the twin dragon.

"We were too slow," Tom said in despair. "Krimon's gone!"

CHAPTER TWO

DRAGON FIRE

Tom ran between the snow-laden trees, calling out to the baby dragon. "Hey! Come back!"

Elenna ran up to him and caught his sleeve. "Shhh!" she hissed. "Listen!"

There was a rustling sound in the trees.

"There!" Elenna yelled, pointing. A moment later, Tom saw Krimon trot into view.

The Beast stopped in front of them, his eyes shining brightly, his head bobbing on his long neck.

"Do you know which way they went?" Tom asked.

The Beast's head tilted, as if he was trying hard to understand what Tom had said. He snorted and a flicker of flame came from his nostrils.

Elenna pointed into the trees. "Show us the way if you can," she said.

Krimon snorted again and turned back the way he had come. He moved off through the trees, trotting along confidently, a low purring growl vibrating in his throat.

The dark trees towered threateningly overhead and shadows crowded around them. Tom gripped his sword – this was no ordinary forest and he had to be on his guard!

Krimon paused on a snow-covered track and lowered his snout, sniffing the ground. Then he closed his eyes and lifted his head. A moment later, long bright flames streamed upwards from his nostrils.

Tom watched in amazement as the tongues of flame hung in the air above the dragon's head, bathing the trees in ruby light, changing shape and weaving together until they became a bright red fireball that turned slowly in the air, hovering between the trees.

"What's he doing?" Elenna asked, backing away from Krimon.

"I don't know," Tom replied. "But look at his chest!" A gentle orange glow was spreading on the red leathery skin, just over where the Beast's heart had to be. As Tom and Elenna watched, the glow deepened

and began to pulse – and in the
centre of the orange light there was
a small circle of emerald green light.
A similar green light shone in the
middle of the hovering fireball.

"It's beautiful," said Elenna. "But
what does it mean?"

"I think it means that there's a bond between the two baby dragons," Tom said. "They're linked in some way." He called to the dragon, "Go on and we'll follow." There was no time to waste – the moon would be rising soon.

With a snort, Krimon plunged into the trees. Tom and Elenna quickly caught up with him. All three of them pushed their way through the undergrowth, snow falling from the branches all around them, the fireball gliding along in front, and the orange and green light throbbing at the Beast's heart. Every now and then they heard a sinister sound, like Malvel's mocking laughter. The deeper they headed into the forest, the darker and more menacing it became.

As Krimon darted this way and that through the trees, Tom saw that sometimes the orange fireball would become dim and the green light would almost disappear. At other times the fireball would glow as brightly as a furnace, and Tom knew that they were heading in the right direction. But time was against them

as the winter daylight faded.

"It will be dark soon," Elenna said, her breath white in the chill air. "We have to find Vedra before nightfall."

"Aduro said the Beasts would be safe until the full moon reached the top of the sky," Tom said urgently. "We're running out of time."

The dragon came to a sudden halt. Ahead of them, a great hedge of holly blocked the way; its branches were as thick as Tom's arms, and its spiky, leathery leaves shone eerily in the reddish light of the hovering fireball.

Tom looked at the prickly, snow-capped hedge. He was sure that it had been deliberately put across their path.

The baby dragon ran distractedly back and forth along the line of the hedge. As far as Tom and Elenna could see, the dense wall of holly stretched on for ever in both directions. Mocking laughter echoed through the shadowy trees.

Krimon stood in front of the hedge.

He lifted his head and let out a long, keening cry. Tom looked at his face and saw that great diamond-bright tears were running from his eyes.

His brother was on the other side of that massive hedge, but there was no way through.

CHAPTER THREE

THE LABYRINTH

Tom drew his sword and stepped up to the towering holly hedge, a grim determination building inside him. He was not going to be stopped from fulfilling his quest. "Not while there is blood in my veins!" he muttered as he gripped his sword in both hands.

He swung with all the strength he had. The sword sliced through leaves and branches, sending them flying.

"Good work, Tom!" Elenna
shouted. She dragged the twigs and
branches away as he stepped
forwards into the hedge, hacking at it
so that splinters of wood and spiky
leaves flew about.

His muscles ached and he was
soon breathing rapidly with the effort
of battling the vicious hedge – but he
could see no end to the tangle of
branches. Behind him he could hear

Krimon snorting encouragement.

At last, he had to pause as exhaustion overcame him. His sword felt unusually heavy, and the muscles in his arms and shoulders were screaming with pain. He lowered his sword, gasping for breath. A feeling of defeat overwhelmed him. "I just don't think I can do it," he said. "I don't know what's wrong with me. I've never felt like this before."

"We'll get through. It'll just take time, that's all."

Tom looked at Elenna. "We don't have time. It's already getting dark," he said. "You know what Aduro told us – if Malvel puts his spell on the dragons when the full moon is at its height, they will be corrupted for ever. They will be evil – and we won't be able to save them."

A snort made them both turn. Krimon was peering at them with sad and lonely eyes. The orange light at his chest was dim and the green circle of fire had almost vanished.

The dragon extended his long neck and gently took the collar of Elenna's tunic in his mouth.

"What's he doing?" she gasped as the dragon drew back, tugging her along with him and making urgent growling noises in his throat. "Hey!

Careful!" she called as she was lifted off her feet and put to one side. "You want us out of the way? Is that it?"

Krimon released her and made a sharp, high-pitched croaking noise.

"Tom!" Elenna called. "Come out of there. I think Krimon has a plan."

Tom stepped out of the hole he had cut in the hedge. The dragon pushed his head into it. Tom saw his sides expand, as though he were taking a deep breath.

A moment later, there was a roaring of fire and a burst of red flame came pouring from the Beast's mouth and nose. Smoke billowed out of the hole and there was a sharp smell of burning. As Krimon moved forwards into the hedge, clumps of snow fell from the upper branches, turning to thick white steam as they hit the flames.

The dragon pushed further into the hole.

"He's burning his way right through!" exclaimed Elenna. "Good work, Krimon!"

Tom and Elenna followed the dragon into the scorched and smouldering hedge. The smoke made them cough, and they could hardly see a thing as they stumbled along behind the Beast, but it was not long before they were through the hedge and breathing fresher air.

Tom wiped his watering eyes with his sleeve. Beyond the barrier of holly, the forest looked quite different. There were no pine trees, just endless parades of snow-laden holly bushes, tall as trees and as dense as the bush they had just fought their way through. Paths led through the ranks of trees, thick with un-trodden snow.

"There are so many different
pathways," Elenna said. She looked
at Krimon, who was staring this way
and that as though he was trying
to find an elusive scent on the air.
The glow on his chest was still pale
and the ball of fire that floated above
his head had gone even dimmer.

Elenna patted the dragon's neck.
"Find him!" she said encouragingly.
"I know you can do it!"

The Beast ran forwards along one
of the many paths. The fireball grew

even fainter. He turned and ran back, following another path. This time the fireball began to glow more brightly.

"That's the way!" Tom said.

Paths led off to the left and right, and sometimes the main path forked so Krimon had to pause for a moment to decide which route to follow. But Tom could see the orange patch glowing bright on his chest, and the circle of green light shining strongly. The fireball was throwing out sparks of red and green light, bright and fierce.

Tom stared up into the sky. The snow clouds were gone and the night was clear – pitch black and sparkling with the cold glitter of winter stars. A deadly chill came creeping through the holly, and Tom was glad to have Nanook the snow monster's enchanted bell on his shield, which protected him against extreme cold. Krimon did not seem to feel the cold, but he saw that Elenna was shivering despite her cloak.

"It can't be long now before the moon rises," he said to her.

"But look how bright the dragon fire is," she replied. "We must be very close."

They came to another fork in the path. Krimon hesitated. A sudden burst of flame ignited close to Tom's head. He jumped back, his shield up and his sword ready in his hand.

Elenna gave a yelp of alarm as another flash of fire appeared on the other side of the pathway. Then more and more fires appeared, igniting one by one all along the path.

"They're torches!" Tom said in amazement, gazing at the long lines of bright lights that hung from the holly branches. "Look – they're everywhere."

"I don't like it," Elenna said. "It's as if the forest has come alive." She frowned. "This is dark magic. These lights aren't here to help us." She turned. "Oh!" She backed away from the hedge.

Tom saw a large dark shape in among the branches. Red eyes glinted. Raised claws and bared fangs gleamed in the torchlight.

"Get back!" Tom shouted, leaping in front of Elenna. A monstrous creature reared above him!

CHAPTER FOUR

THE EVIL CHARM

Tom raised his sword defiantly as the creature loomed over him in the torchlight. It was human-shaped and dark green. Its thick, shiny hide was covered in spikes, its claws were as long as swords and its eyes like boiling blood. But then Tom realised the creature was not moving. Puzzled, he stepped forwards.

"Be careful!" Elenna called.

Tom swung his sword so that the
flat of the blade struck the creature's
leg. There was a resounding clang. Tom
turned, grinning. "It's just a statue!"

Elenna came to stand next to him.
"Nasty looking statue," she remarked.

They saw that the hedges were
filled with many hideous statues,
grown over with holly so that they
were half-hidden.

Krimon was still at the fork in the
maze, growling and whimpering
to himself, his head turning to and fro.

"He doesn't know which way to go,"
Elenna said, walking over to the Beast.

Tom stared along the two pathways.
They were exactly alike. He walked
a little way along the left-hand path.
A thick green mist swirled around his
ankles, rising from the ground beneath

his feet. Sudden, darting pains behind his eyes brought him to a halt.

"What's wrong?" asked Elenna.

"My head feels like it's in a vice!" Tom stumbled back. The moment he reached the fork, the green mist seeped back into the ground and the throbbing in his head faded away.

"I don't think it can be that way," Tom said, staring uneasily along the left-hand path. "At least, I hope it isn't." Suddenly Krimon seemed to make up his mind – and to Tom's relief, he went lumbering down the right-hand path. Tom was sure now that Vedra must be at the heart of this labyrinth.

He stared up at the inky sky. Stars twinkled in the frosty air. The moon had not yet risen – but he feared that at any moment he would see it lifting above the snowy tops of the hedges.

They came to another fork. The
left-hand path was narrow and heavily
overgrown, but the dragon pushed
his way through, the prickly leaves
scraping along his scales, the dislodged
snow trickling down with a soft hiss.

Elenna followed Krimon, with
Tom close behind. But the moment
Tom set foot on the path, a green
mist again billowed up out of the

ground and swirled around his
feet – and his headache returned.

"This can't be the way," he called.
But above the Beast's head the
fireball was pulsing strongly. Elenna
paused, a worried look coming into
her eyes as she saw the mist that
drifted around Tom's feet.

"Krimon thinks it is," she said.
"Is the pain very bad? Don't inhale
any of that mist!"

Tom winced and tried to hold his
breath as the throbbing got worse.
If this was the way, then he would
have to put up with the pain. "Don't
worry about me," he said, hoping he
sounded more confident than he felt.
"Keep close to Krimon. I'll be right
behind you."

Elenna turned and ran after
the Beast, who was moving fast. Tom
screwed up his eyes against the pain,

covering his mouth with his hand, determined not to give up. A soft, low laugh sounded behind him. He turned. A hooded figure stood at the end of the path.

It was Malvel. The evil wizard's laughter rang in Tom's ears. An uncontrollable surge of anger burst through Tom at the sound of that hated voice. With a shout of rage,

he ran back along the path, his shield
up, his sword at the ready.

"Tom! No!" He ignored Elenna's
warning. Malvel was within his
reach. He had the chance to defeat
the evil wizard once and for all.

Malvel stood at the fork in
the paths, his head thrown back as his
laughter rang up into the night sky.
He pointed and laughed again. Tom
followed the line of the pointing

finger. The upper arc of the moon had just cleared the tops of the hedges, the moonlight reflecting eerily on the snow. Time was running out!

Elenna caught hold of Tom and forced him to stop.

"What are you doing, Tom? You're going the wrong way."

Tom thrust his sword in Malvel's direction. "I have to fight him!" he shouted angrily, trying to tear himself away from her.

"Fight who?" Elenna gasped. "Tom? There's no one there."

Tom stared at her. "Are you blind?" he shouted. "Malvel is standing right in front of us!"

"No, he isn't," Elenna insisted. "There's nothing there. It must be the headache and the mist – it's making you see things, Tom."

Tom dragged his arm free of her grip, overcome with an intense anger.

"You need to calm down," Elenna said gently.

Tom realised that he was breathing heavily, almost panting with fury. He had never felt like this before. What was wrong with him? Had Malvel made himself invisible to Elenna – or was she right, and it was just an illusion?

He slowed his breathing and the

anger started to disappear – and the shape of Malvel faded away to nothing.

Tom looked at Elenna. "Thank you," he said quietly. "Malvel must be using that green mist to try to control me. But what do I do if I can't trust my own eyes?"

Elenna took his shoulder. "Trust mine," she said. "Come on – we mustn't let the dragon get away from us."

They ran side by side along the path. The green mist was gone and now Tom's head felt much better.

Krimon was standing still, facing a great dark door that blocked off the path. The young Beast was keening and wailing softly. The door showed scorch marks where the dragon had tried to burn it, but the glossy wood was unharmed by the dragon's fire.

The orange glow was still bright

on his chest, and the fireball flared above his head.

"This has to be the way," Elenna said. "We should look for a key, or some other way to get the door open."

"But there's no handle," Tom said, his anger flaring up again. He lifted his sword in both hands and rushed at the door, smashing again and again at the dark wood. Splinters flew, but the door didn't move.

He thrust at the door with all his might, hammering his shield into the wood, pounding with the hilt of his sword.

"Tom, stop!" Elenna called. "That can't be the way!"

Tom ignored her, letting out a howl of rage as he made one last effort, kicking at the door with all his strength. The door swung open on creaking hinges. Tom glared at Elenna.

"See!" he shouted. "I did it! I knew I could get it open!" Wild elation filled him as he shoved his way through the door. But all that met him was another snow-covered path.

"No!" Tom cried. He ran from side to side, beating at the hedges

with his sword. "I hate this place!"
he screamed.

Krimon backed away from him as
though Tom had become something
to fear.

Elenna darted forwards and caught
Tom's sword-arm. "Get off me!" he
snarled, wrenching his hand free. He
lifted the sword and was about
to bring the blade down on her head
when he looked into her eyes and
realised what he was doing.

With a cry of alarm and horror, Tom stumbled back, throwing his sword down and falling to his knees.

"I'm sorry!" he gasped. "I'm so sorry!"

Elenna knelt in front of him, her hands on his shoulders.

"Look at me, Tom," she said firmly.

He gazed into her eyes, his chest heaving and his limbs shaking.

"This isn't your fault," she said. "Something has been done to you. It's making you behave in this way." Tom saw fear in her eyes.

"Tom – I think that the dust Seth threw in your eyes has put you under an evil charm. You have to fight it, Tom. You have to fight it really hard – if you don't, then Malvel will win."

Tom could barely speak. He didn't know what to do. This quest was too hard. Everything felt hopeless.

CHAPTER FIVE

THE CHASM

"I can't control myself," he said. "Malvel's magic is too strong! I can't beat him, Elenna. I can't!"

"You have to try," Elenna said. "I'll help you."

"But you don't understand – I might attack you."

"You think you can beat me, do you?" Elenna said, arching an eyebrow. "Don't be so sure!"

Krimon was still eyeing Tom nervously, as though he could sense the evil charm. "Don't be scared, I'm better now," Tom said, hoping that he would be able to control his rage.

"Come along," Elenna called to the Beast. "Let's go and find your brother!"

With a snort, Krimon pushed though the open doorway and went trotting along the path.

Following, Tom glanced up at the sky. Half of the full moon was now visible over the holly hedges. They had so little time.

They had not been going for long before they came to a wide chasm that stretched across their path. Krimon stood at the edge, peering over to the far side.

Tom stared down into the chasm.

It was very deep, and far, far below them he could see flames flickering. He knew that the eagle feather in his shield which Arcta the mountain giant had given him would protect him from a fall, but it would be no help to Elenna.

"We have to get across," he said.

"I know. But how?"

While they were still wondering

what to do, the dragon took a few steps backwards and then leaped across the chasm. His wings spread as he landed safely on the far side. He turned, looking back at them.

"Come back!" Tom called. "You can carry us over."

Krimon snorted and let out a belch of flame. He clawed at the ground and turned his head, indicating that

he wanted them to follow.

"It's too far for us!" Elenna called. "You'll have to jump back and help us."

But Krimon did not understand – he just stood there watching them with confused eyes. Tom felt the sting of tears. He wished that they had not left Epos and Ferno behind; the two grown Beasts could easily have carried them over the chasm on their backs.

Tom fought hard to keep down his anger. It wasn't the baby dragon's fault. But they had to get across.

A thought struck Tom. "If we had a pole, we could vault over," he said.

"A branch from one of those enormous hedges might work," Elenna agreed eagerly.

Tom ran to the giant hedge and hacked at it with his sword. He sliced off the smaller twigs and branches

from one long limb, cutting it free and
dragging it onto the path. He trimmed
the long branch so that it became
a smooth pole twice his own height.
He tested it. It seemed flexible

enough not to break. "I'll go first," he said. "Then I'll throw it back for you."

He lifted the pole, rested it on his shoulder and took several steps backwards, his eyes fixed firmly on the far side of the chasm. He ran forwards. The pole hit the ground. It slipped a little on the snow, then held firm. Tom sprang into the air, twisting in mid-flight, propelling himself forwards. He hung in the air over the chasm, glancing fearfully down to see the deep gulf gaping open to swallow him. He gave a final jerk of his hips, the balance shifted and he was safely on the other side.

He threw the pole back to Elenna and she caught it easily. A few moments later she was at his side.

"Let's hope that was the last obstacle," she said.

They walked on, but Tom quickly

noticed that something was wrong with Krimon.

The Beast would falter every now and then, lifting a foreleg and rubbing at his neck with his claw, whining as if in pain. As they went on, Krimon got more and more distressed until finally, at a place from which seven paths led off, he fell to the ground, tearing and scratching frantically at his neck.

"What's wrong with him?" Elenna asked.

Tom ran forwards and fell to his knees beside the writhing dragon. "It must be the link to his brother," Tom said, panic rising in him. "Something bad must be happening to Vedra." He looked at Elenna. "He's suffering the same pain!"

The dragon thrashed about on the ground, crying out in agony. Above the maze of hedges, the moon was

rising in the sky, its cold light giving the snow a ghostly sheen.

Suddenly the fireball over Krimon's head sputtered and went out, and at the same moment the orange glow on his chest disappeared. The Beast stopped writhing. He lay panting for a few moments, then got to his feet. Tom saw the look of loneliness in his eyes. Krimon began to whimper, thrusting his huge head into Elenna's

shoulder, fat tears running from his eyes as she wrapped her arms around him.

"The link between Vedra and Krimon has been broken," Tom said. "Something very bad must have happened to his brother." He felt desperate. He had failed. This really was the end – without the dragon to guide them, how would they ever get into the heart of the maze?

CHAPTER SIX

THE HEART OF
THE MAZE

"What are we going to do?" Elenna
asked. Tom could see tears shining
in her eyes as she cradled the Beast.

"Why ask me?" he snapped. "I'm
not a wizard who knows everything!"

Elenna bit her lip.

"I'm sorry," he said, breathing
deeply. He knew he had to fight
against this strange anger that came

from Malvel's evil magic. It would only cloud his mind and make things more difficult. But the whimpering of Krimon was making his head ache even more.

The dragon cried out again. Tom turned on the Beast, shaking, his hand on his sword hilt as he glared at him. "Be quiet!"

"Tom, he isn't making a sound," Elenna said.

Tom stared at her. "I can hear him," he said. "He's howling and moaning."

"No, he isn't."

Tom looked at Krimon. She was right. Then where could the whimpering and crying out be coming from? His head cleared for a moment and sudden understanding dawned.

"It's Vedra!" he gasped.

"I can't hear anything," Elenna said.

"I can – listen closely. There!" Tom said.

He stared around the junction of the seven paths. Facing one of them, he heard Vedra's cries grow a little louder in his head.

"He's this way!" he said. "Come on – try to get Krimon to follow."

Tom ran down the path, filled with new faith in himself. Malvel had put an evil charm on him to try to make him fail – and now that same charm was leading him to the quest's end.

Elenna and Krimon followed as Tom ran through the maze, kicking up clumps of snow as he went. His breath was white smoke in the freezing night air. Vedra's voice was loud in his ears now – the lost Beast was very close.

The full moon had risen above the hedges and was shining down into the labyrinth of snow-laden holly trees. But they still had a little while before it reached the top of the sky. Time to succeed…or time to fail.

Tom came to a fork in the maze.

"I can hear him now," Elenna cried, coming up behind him as he hesitated at the junction.

With Tom in the lead, they turned a final bend and came stumbling into a wide circular clearing. Vedra was there in the centre – pinned to the ground by thick spiked chains

of gold. As the Beast struggled, the
spikes tore his flesh, and Tom saw
that the injuries were worst around
Vedra's neck, where threads of
blood ran down his shining scales.

Tom realised that these must be
the injuries Krimon had felt when he
shed tears for his twin.

Standing just out of the reach of
the green dragon was Seth. The boy
smiled as Tom, Elenna and Krimon
came into the clearing.

"I see you have come to watch
the full moon with us," Seth said
with a mocking bow. "My master
hoped you would be here in time
to see the Beasts corrupted."

Tom was about to launch himself at
the smirking boy, when Krimon ran
past him towards his captive twin.

To Tom's surprise, Seth took
a sudden sidestep towards Vedra and
jerked at the end of his chains. The
golden links fell away from the Beast
and he rose from the ground.

But Tom saw an evil light in
the green dragon's eyes. Something

had happened to it. As his twin ran
forwards, Vedra reared up, his eyes
gleaming with wicked magic. His
jaws opened and a burst of fierce fire
spurted towards the red dragon. A
moment later, the green dragon
leaped at his twin, roaring with
anger, his jaws wide, his claws raised.

Malvel's dark magic was in Vedra's blood – he had already been turned to evil. Tom was too late.

CHAPTER SEVEN

THE FULL MOON

With a cry of rage, Tom rushed towards Vedra to stop him from attacking his twin.

But Seth sprang forwards, his bronze sword whirling in the moonlight. "You can't do anything now. Vedra is ours!"

"Try fighting me one-on-one," Tom challenged his opponent. "No magic tricks."

Seth grinned, his face pure evil. "I don't need magic to defeat you." Quick as a snake, Seth struck out with his bronze sword and sent Tom's blade leaping from his hand.

Tom fell back as blow after savage blow rained down on his shield. He stumbled and fell onto his side in the snow, just managing to keep his shield up. Over to one side, he could see Vedra and Krimon engaged in their own savage fight.

Seth straddled Tom, his sword rising and falling. Tom felt his arm muscles weakening under the savage blows. He could not think properly – his mind was clouded with despair, and he felt that defeat was not far away.

Then he heard a high-pitched yell, and above the rim of his shield he saw Elenna attacking Seth from the side, wielding Tom's own sword, beating him back, trading blow for blow as she forced him away from Tom.

But even as Tom tried to get to his feet, he saw that Elenna's attack was failing. Seth was too strong for her. He was fighting back with hard and fast blows.

Using all his strength, Tom hurled his shield at Seth, skimming it just above the ground. It caught Seth right below the knees, sending him crashing to the ground.

Elenna was quick to take advantage of their enemy's fall. She brought her foot down on his wrist, stooping to snatch the bronze sword from his fingers.

"Well done, Elenna!" Tom shouted, scrambling to his feet.

"I've got him," Elenna called. "Take this – help Krimon!" She threw Tom his sword, transferring Seth's bronze sword to her right hand and aiming the point squarely at the boy's throat. Seth glared up at her but didn't try to move.

The noise of the fighting twin dragons was terrifying. Their roars filled the clearing as tails lashed and flame spurted and claws lunged. Vedra was winning the battle – the

evil inside him was making him fight
more fiercely. As Tom ran forwards,
he saw Krimon tumble onto his back
with a howl.

Vedra pounced on his twin with
a blast of fire. The snow turned
to spurting steam all around them. If
Krimon had not been covered in
fire-proof scales, he would have been
scorched to death by the blast of flame.

The fact that Vedra's attention was focused on his brother was Tom's only advantage. He knew what he had to do, and with the moon high in the sky he had only a few seconds left to do it. He remembered Aduro's words. He had to score Vedra's underbelly with the tip of his enchanted sword, marking him with the sign of good. And he had to do it before the possessed Beast noticed him.

He ran in close, looking for a way to get in under the green dragon's scaly sides. It was impossible! The soft under-parts were too well protected.

The moon was a hand's-breadth from the top of the sky. Tom stared up at the silver disc for a moment, a plan forming in his mind. He hadn't come so far to give up now.

"Hey!" he shouted above the roaring of the dragons. He struck

Vedra's foreleg with his sword. The
metal rang uselessly on the emerald
scales, but the green dragon's fiery
eyes turned towards him.

He leaped aside as a blast of flame
burned the ground where he had
been standing. He had to act quickly.

He angled his silver sword, tilting it just so – holding its surface up to the sky so that the reflection of the full moon was caught on its shining blade.

He tilted it a little more, seeing a flash of brilliant silver light strike Vedra in the eyes. Dazzled and blinded, the Beast reared up, his wings stretching wide. His jaws opened to spew a fountain of flame into the night sky.

Tom did not hesitate. He sprang

forwards, seeing the soft belly of
the dragon revealed. He used the
very tip of his sword, carefully
scoring the yielding flesh.

"No!" Seth howled in anger, but in
an instant his voice was swallowed
by a whirling sound like a thousand
hurricanes.

Tom stood firm, his eyes blinded
by the racing winds that blasted
across the clearing, his ears filled
with the noise.

And then there was a long, deep silence. Tom opened his eyes. The maze of towering holly bushes was gone. He was standing on a plateau of deep, smooth snow. Vedra and Krimon were beside him, blinking and shaking their heads in confusion. Elenna was nearby, but Seth and the bronze sword were gone.

"You did it!" Elenna shouted.

"We did it!" Tom said with a grin.

The twin Beasts were recovering now, rubbing fondly against one another and crooning. Vedra was cured of the evil – he would carry the mark of good on his belly for ever, and Malvel's power would never be able to harm him again.

But Tom knew this wasn't his last battle with the evil wizard – Malvel would return with some fresh evil!

Laughing with joy, Elenna ran up to

the dragons. "You're safe now!" she
called to them. She looked at Tom.
"Do you think they understand what
we did for them?"

"I'm sure they do," Tom said. "But
what do we do now? Where exactly
are we?"

"Check the map," Elenna said.

Tom brought the magic map out of his tunic and unrolled it. A golden dot showed where they were. "We're in the middle of nowhere!" Tom groaned. "How are we going to get back home without Epos and Ferno?"

"We won't have to," Elenna said. "Look!" She pointed into the southern sky. Tom saw with a jolt of relief that Ferno and Epos were winging their way towards them over the snowy forest.

"Well done, Beasts!" Tom shouted, waving to the creatures as they drew closer. "We'll get to ride home after all!"

Vedra and Krimon gave deep welcoming grunts as Ferno and Epos landed gracefully on the snowy plateau. Tom ran towards Epos.

"You're better!" he called. "I'm so glad!"

Epos cawed loudly, her wings reflecting the moonlight as she spread them to show she was fully recovered. Ferno lumbered towards the twin dragons, his eyes shining kindly. Their wings flapped and their heads bobbed as they rubbed against the Beast's huge sides.

Ferno made a series of low, rumbling noises and Vedra and Krimon began to climb up onto his back.

"He must be telling them something,"

Elenna said. "I wonder what."

"I think he's letting them know that he's going to take them somewhere where they can grow up safely – somewhere in the mountains of Rion."

The great dragon took to the air, the twins clinging to his back as he rose in majestic spirals up into the night sky. He turned, his black silhouette flying across the face of the moon as he headed north into the mountains.

"Epos? Will you take us home?"
Tom asked the waiting bird.

Epos cawed loudly.

Tom looked again at the map, and saw a golden thread spinning out southwards across Rion and down into Avantia – showing them the way home.

A moment later, a shimmering face appeared on the map. It was Aduro the wizard, and he was smiling.

"Well done, my brave friends," he said, his voice echoing as if it was coming from many miles away. "And you are right, Tom – Ferno will take the twins to a place of safety. He will remain by their side and teach them the ways of good and protect them until they grow strong. Now, my friends, climb up onto Epos's back and come home to the palace."

"We've won the fight against

Malvel," Elenna said sadly. "But I've lost my bow and arrows."

"Fear not – I retrieved them from the volcano with my magic," the wizard said. "They are waiting for you in the palace."

Elenna gave a yell of delight as Aduro's face faded away.

Tom rolled up the map and he and Elenna climbed onto Epos's warm and feathered back. Tom felt exhausted but he was in high spirits.

He clung on tightly as the bird launched herself into the night sky.

"I wonder how Storm and Silver have been managing without us," Elenna said.

"They'll be disappointed to have missed the quest!" Tom replied with a smile.

"We'll tell them all about it as soon as we get back," Elenna said.

Cool winds blew through Tom's hair as they sped southwards over a snowy landscape that shone like silver under the full moon. He smiled. He had succeeded in his quest and the twin Beasts of Avantia were safe. He didn't know if he would ever see Vedra and Krimon again, but at least there were two new Beasts who would be taught how to protect the kingdom; two pure and noble Beasts to join the battle against Malvel. And as for Seth…? Tom shivered, wondering if they would meet again. Only time would tell.

But for now, Tom was going home. Home to Avantia.

JOIN TOM ON HIS NEXT BEAST QUEST SOON!

Win an exclusive
Beast Quest T-shirt and goody bag!

In every Beast Quest book the Beast Quest logo is
hidden in one of the pictures. Find the logos in books
55 to 60 and make a note of which pages they appear
on. Write the six page numbers on a postcard and
send it in to us.
Each month we will draw one winner to receive
a Beast Quest T-shirt and goody bag.

THE BEAST QUEST COMPETITION:
THE MASTER OF THE BEASTS
Orchard Books
338 Euston Road, London NW1 3BH
Australian readers should email:
childrens.books@hachette.com.au

New Zealand readers should write to:
Beast Quest Competition
4 Whetu Place, Mairangi Bay, Auckland, NZ
or email: childrensbooks@hachette.co.nz

Only one entry per child.
Final draw: 4 March 2013

You can also enter this competition
via the Beast Quest website: www.beastquest.co.uk

Join the Quest,
Join the Tribe

www.beastquest.co.uk

Have you checked out the Beast Quest website?
It's the place to go for games, downloads, activities,
sneak previews and lots of fun!

You can read all about your favourite Beasts, down-
load free screensavers and desktop wallpapers for
your computer, and even challenge your friends
to a Beast Tournament.

Sign up to the newsletter at www.beastquest.co.uk
to receive exclusive extra content and the oppor-
tunity to enter special members-only competitions.
We'll send you up-to-date info on all the Beast
Quest books, including the next exciting series
which features six brand-new Beasts!

Get 30% off all Beast Quest Books at www.beastquest.co.uk
Enter the code BEAST at the checkout.

Offer valid in UK and ROI, offer expires December 2013

All books priced at £4.99,
special bumper editions
priced at £5.99.

Orchard Books are available from all good bookshops, or can
be ordered from our website: www.orchardbooks.co.uk,
or telephone 01235 827702, or fax 01235 8227703.